Lexile __300L__

Accelerated Reader

Book Level __1.3__ AR Pts __0.5__

TALES
OF
OLIVER PIG

TALES
OF
OLIVER PIG

Jean Van Leeuwen
PICTURES BY
ARNOLD LOBEL

THE DIAL PRESS · NEW YORK

Published by
The Dial Press
1 Dag Hammarskjold Plaza
New York, New York 10017

Text copyright ©1979 by Jean Van Leeuwen
Pictures copyright ©1979 by Arnold Lobel
All rights reserved. Manufactured in the U.S.A.
First Printing

Library of Congress Cataloging in Publication Data
Van Leeuwen, Jean. Tales of Oliver Pig.
Summary: Five adventures of Oliver Pig with his family.
[1. Pigs—Fiction. 2. Family life—Fiction]
I. Lobel, Arnold. II. Title.
PZ7.V3273Tal [E] 79-4276
ISBN 0-8037-8736-7 lib. bdg.
ISBN 0-8037-8737-5 pbk.

The art is prepared in black line
with gray, yellow, and red washes,
all of which are reproduced as halftone.

For David,
the real Oliver Pig

CONTENTS

BAKING DAY

"Today," said Oliver,

"I want to dig a very deep hole.

And after that

I will make you a sand cake."

"Today is not a day for outside,"

said Mother.

"It is cold and wet."

"What can I do then?" asked Oliver.

"Come to the kitchen,"
said Mother.
A big yellow mixing bowl
was on the kitchen table.
"Today," said Mother,
"is a baking day."
"What are we going to bake?"
asked Oliver.
"Oatmeal cookies," said Mother.
"With raisins?" asked Oliver.

"With lots of raisins,"
said Mother.

Mother took the cooking things
out of the cupboard.
"What will we put
in the cookies?"
asked Oliver.
"First some butter," said Mother.
"And some sugar."

"Can I do the mixing?" asked Oliver.

"Yes," said Mother.

Oliver started stirring.

"Gah?" said Amanda.

Mother gave Amanda

a bowl and spoon.

Amanda started stirring.

"Now we'll need an egg," said Mother.

Oliver stirred up the egg

until the yellow part disappeared.

"And the oats, of course,"

said Mother.

Oliver stirred them in.

"And a cup of flour

and some baking powder," said Mother.

Oliver stirred and stirred.

Flour spilled on the table.

Flour got all over Oliver.

"This is hard work," said Oliver.

"Yes," said Mother.

"But you are a good helper."

Amanda patted flour

all over herself.

"Now the spices," said Mother.

Oliver put in a sprinkle of nutmeg

and a sprinkle of cloves

and two sprinkles of cinnamon.

"We need one thing more,"

said Mother.

"What do you think it is?"

"Raisins?" asked Oliver.

"Raisins," said Mother.

Mother poured two piles of raisins

on the table.

"These are for the cookies,"
she said,
"and these are for my helper."
"Gah?" said Amanda.
Mother poured two piles of raisins
on Amanda's tray.
Amanda ate both piles.
"Now the cookie dough is ready,"
said Mother.

Oliver patted the dough

into little balls.

Mother put them in the pan.

"What comes next?" asked Oliver.

"The baking is next," said Mother.

Mother put the cookies
into the oven.
"What would you like to do
while the cookies bake?"
she asked.
"Let's do nothing," said Oliver.
"Let's just wait to eat some."
Mother and Oliver and Amanda
sat at the kitchen table.
They listened
to the rain outside.
They smelled the smell
of baking cookies.

"I am happy now," said Oliver.

"Why are you happy?" asked Mother.

"Because you are here," said Oliver.

"And Amanda is here.

And I am not cold and wet,

I am warm.

Baking cookies is warm."

"That is what I like

about a baking day," said Mother.

A BAD DAY

"I am building a road," said Oliver.

"And Amanda can't touch anything."

Oliver's road went

across the whole couch.

It had bridges and tunnels

and a gas station

and a parking lot.

He put his cars and trucks on it.

"Now they are all parked," he said,

"and it's a traffic jam."

Amanda picked up Oliver's racing car.

"No!" said Oliver.

Amanda began to cry.

"Oliver," said Father,

"wouldn't it be nice

to let Amanda play with one car?"

"No," said Oliver.

"All my cars are for me."

After lunch Oliver took down

his dinosaur book.

"Read to me," he said.

Father and Oliver

read together

in the big chair.

Amanda read on the floor.

Oliver got down

and took Amanda's book.

"I want to read this book," he said.

Amanda began to cry.

"Oliver," said Father,

"wouldn't it be nice

to share the books?"

"No," said Oliver.

"The books are mine."

After he finished reading,

Oliver dumped out all his blocks.

"I am going to build a skyscraper,"

he said.

"It will be twenty stories high.

Amanda, go away."

Oliver started building.

Amanda watched.

The skyscraper got very tall.

Amanda stood on tiptoe

to put a block on top.

"No!" said Oliver.

He took it off.

The skyscraper fell down.

"No, no, no, no, no!" shouted Oliver.

Amanda began to cry.

Father hugged them both.

"She made my skyscraper fall down,"
said Oliver.

"She was only trying to help,"
said Father. "Isn't it nice
to help each other?"

"No," said Oliver. "It isn't nice."

"You and Amanda have had a bad day,"
said Father.

"Maybe some supper will help."
On the table were
spaghetti and meatballs
and peas and bread and butter.
"This is my best supper," said Oliver.
"Put a lot on my plate."
Father and Mother and Oliver
began to eat.
Amanda didn't.
"Open your mouth
and close your eyes,"
said Father.

"And I will give you
a scrumptious surprise."
Amanda opened her mouth
and closed her eyes.
Father put a meatball in.

Amanda spit it out.

"Maybe she is cutting her molars,"

said Mother.

Oliver had two peas left.

He put one in his mouth.

"Mmm, yummy," he said.

He put the other pea

on Amanda's plate.

Amanda looked at Oliver.

She ate the pea.

Oliver put a piece of spaghetti
on Amanda's plate.

Amanda ate it.

Oliver put a meatball
on Amanda's plate.

"Ummy," said Amanda,
and she ate it all.

"My goodness," said Father,

"I believe Oliver has discovered

the secret of getting

Amanda to eat."

"I believe he has," said Mother.

Oliver laughed.

Amanda laughed.

Then Oliver gave Amanda

the bread and butter

he was saving on his plate for last.

GRANDMOTHER'S VISIT

"Is there any mail for me?"

asked Oliver.

Mother took the letters

out of the mailbox.

"Here is a letter

for The Benjamin Pig Family,"

she said.

"Does Family mean me?" asked Oliver.

"Yes," said Mother.

Mother and Oliver and Amanda
read the letter. It said,
"My dears: I am delighted
that you asked me to visit.
I will be there on Thursday
in time for supper.
Love, Grandmother."
"Oh, my," said Mother.
"Today is Thursday.
I will have to work hard
to get ready for Grandmother."

"I will work hard with you,"
said Oliver.

"First we will clean
Grandmother's room,"
said Mother.

Mother dusted the floor.

Oliver dusted the tables.

Amanda dusted under the bed
with her stomach.
She found the missing piece
from Oliver's puzzle.
"Some flowers on the table
would be nice," said Mother.
Oliver and Amanda picked pansies
from the garden.
Mother put them
next to Grandmother's bed.

"Grandmother likes to read in bed,"
said Mother.

She put an extra pillow on the bed.

Oliver got his monster book
and his elephant.

"Grandmother can read
my monster book," he said.

"And she can hug my elephant
when she goes to sleep."

"That is nice," said Mother.

"Now Grandmother's

room is ready.

After lunch

I will start the cooking."

Oliver watched Mother cook.

"What are you making?"

he asked.

"Cherry pie," said Mother.

"It is a surprise for Grandmother."

"I want to make a surprise

for Grandmother too,"

said Oliver.

Oliver went to his room
and mixed up a raisin pie
and put it in the oven.
Then he cooked some other things
for Grandmother.

He made spaghetti and meatballs
and cinnamon toast
and chocolate pudding
and apple juice.
"Now I am ready for Grandmother,"
he said.
Grandmother came a little later.
When she saw her room, she said,
"Everything is just right."

"Supper is ready," said Mother.

"Good," said Grandmother.

"I am hungry as a bear."

They sat down at the table.

"Cherry pie," said Grandmother.

"What a lovely surprise."

"I made you a lovely surprise too,"

said Oliver. "It is a raisin pie."

"I am very fond of raisin pie,"

said Grandmother.

After supper

Oliver took Grandmother

to his room.

She sat at his table

and ate spaghetti and meatballs

and cinnamon toast

and chocolate pudding

and apple juice and raisin pie.

Then she rocked

in the rocking chair

with Oliver and Amanda

on her lap.

"Are you still hungry as a bear,
Grandmother?" asked Oliver.
"No," said Grandmother.
"With cherry pie
and raisin pie to eat
and you and Amanda to hug,
I am full right up to the top."
"Me too," said Oliver.

SNOWSUITS

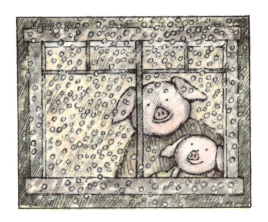

Oliver saw the snow coming down.

"I want to sit on top

of a big pile of snow," he said.

"And I want you

to pull me on my sled.

And I want to make footprints."

"All right," said Mother.

"Let's get ready."

Mother got out

the snowsuits.

Oliver got out his sweater

that Grandmother made.

Amanda got out

all her sweaters.

"No, no," said Mother.

She put the sweaters away.

Mother helped Oliver

with his snowsuit

and his scarf and his hat.

She started on his boots.

Amanda got out her boots

and all of her hats.

"No, no," said Mother.

She put the extra hats away.

"Look," said Oliver,

"I put on my boots myself."

"Very good," said Mother.

Mother put on Amanda's sweater

and her snowsuit and her scarf.

"Mother," said Oliver,

"I can't walk in my boots."

"Your boots are on the wrong feet,"

said Mother. "Let me help you."

Amanda put on her hat.

It covered her eyes.

"No, no," said Mother.

"Come here, Amanda."

Amanda couldn't see to come here.

She fell down.

Her snowsuit made her

too fat to get up.

She began to cry.

"Don't cry, my sweet potato,"

said Mother.

She gave Amanda a kiss.

Amanda stopped crying.

Mother started on Amanda's boots.

Oliver got out his pail and shovel

and his dump truck

and his steam shovel.

"Oliver," said Mother,

"those are sand toys,

not snow toys."

Amanda got out

her stuffed rabbit

and her pull duck.

"No, no," said Mother.

"Those are not snow toys either."

Mother put all the toys away.

"Now I will help you

with your mittens,"

she said.

"I can do mine myself,"
said Oliver.

"Very good," said Mother.

"Look," said Oliver,

"I put my mittens
on my ears."

"Oliver, you know that mittens
don't go on ears," said Mother.
She fixed Oliver's mittens.

Then she lifted

Oliver and Amanda

into the big chair.

"Now see if you can sit very still,"

she said,

"while I put on my coat and hat."

When Mother came back,

Oliver and Amanda

were sitting very still.

But Oliver's hat

and scarf and mittens

and Amanda's hat

and scarf and mittens

were on the floor.

"What happened?" asked Mother.

"We got too hot," said Oliver.

Mother sat very still on the couch.

"What are you doing?" asked Oliver.

"I am crying," said Mother.

"You can't cry," said Oliver.

"Mothers don't cry."

"Well, I am," said Mother.

Oliver climbed into Mother's lap.

"Don't cry, sweet potato," he said.

"We will be nice."

Amanda gave Mother a kiss.

Mother dried her eyes.

"I am finished crying," she said.

"Let's go outside."

"Hooray!" said Oliver.

"I will sit on top of the snow."

"Bye-bye," said Amanda.

IS IT OLIVER?

"I am hiding," said Oliver.

"Come and find me."

Father came in the room.

He looked in the closet.

He looked in the toy box.

He looked under the bed.

"I can't find Oliver anywhere,"

he said.

He looked in the bed.

"Aha!" said Father.

"What is this I see
with only its ears sticking out?
Is it a big brown bear?"

"No," said Oliver.

"Well, then," said Father,
"could these be the ears
of an elephant?"

"No," said Oliver.

"I know," said Father,
"a mouse has crept
into my house."
"No," said Oliver.

"Maybe," said Father,

"it's a caterpillar."

"No," said Oliver.

"Or a cucumber," said Father.

"No," said Oliver.

"I've got it," said Father,

"it's a steam shovel."

"No," said Oliver.

"There is only one thing left,"
said Father.

"It must be a meatball."

"No," said Oliver.

"I give up then," said Father.

"What can it be? Please tell me."

"It's your Oliver," said Oliver.
Father lifted the quilt
from Oliver's face.
"Why so it is," he said.
Father gave Oliver
a hug and a kiss
and tucked him in tight.

"Good night, my little Oliver,"
he said.

"Good night, Father," said Oliver.

And he went right to sleep.